This Walker book belongs to:

_____

_____

_____

First published 1986 by Walker Books Ltd
87 Vauxhall Walk, London SE11 5HJ

This edition published 2015

2 4 6 8 10 9 7 5 3 1

This book has been typeset in Optima

Printed in China

British Library Cataloguing in Publication Data:
a catalogue record for this book is available from the British Library

ISBN 978-1-4063-6749-2

www.walker.co.uk

"Have you seen the crocodile?"

Colin West

WALKER BOOKS

AND SUBSIDIARIES

LONDON • BOSTON • SYDNEY • AUCKLAND

"Have you seen the crocodile?"
asked the parrot.

"No," said the dragonfly.

"Have you seen the crocodile?"
asked the parrot
and the dragonfly.

"No,"
said the
bumble bee.

"Have you seen the crocodile?"
asked the parrot
and the dragonfly
and the bumble bee.

"No,"
said the
butterfly.

"Have you seen the crocodile?"
asked the parrot
and the dragonfly
and the bumble bee
and the butterfly.

"No,"
said the
hummingbird.

"Have you seen the crocodile?"
asked the parrot
and the dragonfly
and the bumble bee
and the butterfly
and the hummingbird.

"No," said the frog.

"No one's seen the crocodile?"
said the parrot
and the dragonfly
and the bumble bee
and the butterfly
and the hummingbird
and the frog.

But then...

"I'VE SEEN THE CROCODILE!" snapped the crocodile.

"Have YOU seen the parrot
and the dragonfly
and the bumble bee
and the butterfly
and the hummingbird
and the frog?"

asked the crocodile.

Colin West says of the last picture in *"Have You Seen the Crocodile?"*,
"The crocodile looks very pleased with himself, but I wonder
if all the other animals escaped being gobbled up?
In the previous picture, they seem to be doing a good job
of escaping! By the way, did you spot the little frog
hiding amongst the lily pads in the endpapers?"